BLACK WOMEN OF THE OLD WEST

Atheneum Books By William Loren Katz

BLACK INDIANS

THE LINCOLN BRIGADE *(WITH MARC CRAWFORD)*

BREAKING THE CHAINS

PROUDLY RED AND BLACK *(WITH PAULA FRANKLIN)*

BLACK WOMEN OF THE OLD WEST

BLACK WOMEN OF THE OLD WEST

WILLIAM LOREN KATZ

ILLUSTRATED WITH ARCHIVAL PHOTOGRAPHS AND PRINTS

ATHENEUM BOOKS FOR YOUNG READERS

Atheneum Books for Young Readers
An imprint of Simon and Schuster Children's Publishing Division
1230 Avenue of the Americas
New York, New York 10020

Designed by Brian Mulligan
The text of this book is set in Goudy and Goudy Sans

Printed in Hong Kong
10 9 8 7 6 5 4 3
First Edition

Library of Congress Cataloging-in-Publication Data
Katz, William Loren.
Black women of the Old West / by William Loren Katz.
p. cm.
"Illustrated with prints and photographs."
ISBN 0-689-31944-4
1. Afro-American women pioneers—West (U.S.)—History—
Juvenile literature. I. Title.
E185.925.K375 1995   95-9969
978'.00496073'0082—dc20   CIP
                                 AC

HALFTITLE PAGE:

Left: Pioneer Nebraskan Mrs. John Adams stares solemnly into a frontier camera. Nebraska State Historical Society

Center: Leona Duncan Matthews in the early 20th-century southwest. Richardson Collection

Right: In 1910 Mrs. Frank Faucett was a church worker in the southwest. Richardson Collection

TITLE PAGE:

Goldie Walker Hayes and her husband, Roy, at their Nebraska farm. William Loren Katz Collection

PART ONE, PIONEERS OF THE SLAVE ERA:

Slaves fled to freedom by land and sea, and were ruthlessly pursued as depicted in this abolitionist drawing. William Loren Katz Collection

PART TWO, WESTWARD TO FREEDOM:

Women, children, and men walked to Kansas up the Chisolm Trail in 1879, as this sketch from *Harper's Weekly* in August shows. Kansas Historical Society, William Loren Katz Collection

ACKNOWLEDGMENTS

After a lifetime of researching and writing in the field of African-American western history, it is difficult to remember all who aided in the completion of this book. Some helped years or decades ago when the project was not even a concrete book idea. I certainly owe an enormous debt for the contributions made over many years by a host of western African-American women historians: Barbara Richardson of Tucson, Arizona, who generously made available her photograph collection of southwestern women of color; Bertha Calloway, curator of the Great Plains Black History Museum; editor Rose Davis of Las Vegas, Nevada; Esther Mumford, the premier scholar of black Seattle; and my dear friend, the late Dr. Sara Dunlop Jackson of the National Archives, who as usual prodded me onward and, I believe, had her great spirit help me complete this book.

In this project, I was able to exchange views with some scholars whose work I had previously admired from afar, particularly pioneer women historians Professor Glenda Ri-ley and Professor Ann Butler. I also have to thank such stalwart supporters as Dr. Gloria Joseph of the Virgin Islands, Gloria Lowrey Turrell of Queens, writer Mary Kay Penn, film documentarians Mirra Bank and Sam Pollard, educators Dr. Laurie Lehman and Dr. Donna Elam, scholar/writer Andrea Pinkney, historian Herb Boyd, my faithful editor Marcia Marshall, museum curator Vivian Ayers-Allen, Dr. John Hope Franklin, writer Josie Gregoire, Dr. Gerald Horne, editor Esther Jackson, Dwayne Key of Atlanta, Joan Waite of New Jersey, director of the Harlem Arts Center, Greg Mills, Chief Osceola Townsend of the Mattinecock nation, and writer George Tooks.

Despite the advice, leads, and enthusiasm proffered by so many, I assume responsibility for any errors of fact and judgment in the book. I hope the fascinating American story that begins to unfold in these pages will attract other researchers who also believe that the truth will make us free.

CONTENTS

WESTWARD TO FREEDOM

The Shore family, homesteaders in Custer County, Nebraska, in the late 1880s, pose in front of their sod house, proudly displaying their new baby and the family dog. William Loren Katz Collection

INTRODUCTION

African-American women appear in few textbooks and in few Hollywood or TV movies of the West, but they were likely to turn up anywhere in American frontier life. Thousands, welcomed by or born among Native American nations, tried to help stave off the march of white "manifest destiny."

Many were devoted mothers, daughters, or wives burdened by their labors and often oppressed by bigotry. They were loyal to their families, churches, and communities. Often, a young wife gave birth by candlelight in a crude log cabin, prairie shack, or sod house. Under primitive frontier circumstances, many died in the effort.

Most led ordinary, hardworking lives in the nineteenth century, but not all. One drove a stagecoach and delivered the U.S. mail in Cascade, Montana. One, sitting on the back seat of the Marysville-Comptonville stagecoach, died

Southwestern pioneer Sarah Montgomery, whose occupation was housecleaning, and whose great interest was African-American folklore. (1880) Richardson Collection

Cathy Williams was hard to stop. As
William Cathy she served from 1868–1870
in the Buffalo Soldiers and won a decoration.
She later ran a farm in the southwest.
Richardson Collection

Ute Kitty Cloud Taylor,
wife of cow puncher
John Taylor, stands in
back of her child and
next to her sister and
her child. Denver
Public Library
Western Collection

in a blaze of gunfire during California's first stagecoach robbery. Another, in early Seattle, helped her husband run a newspaper. In early Texas, another started an impassioned crusade to elevate women and liberate the workers of the world.

An African-American woman owned Beverly Hills, California, and another owned huge parcels of Los Angeles real estate; one founded a black town in Oklahoma; another ran a large carting business in Nevada; and the funeral of another was conducted by the Colorado Pioneers Association

African-American Grant Chapel in the southwest and some of the congregation with the Reverend John Turner (in rear with beard). Richardson Collection

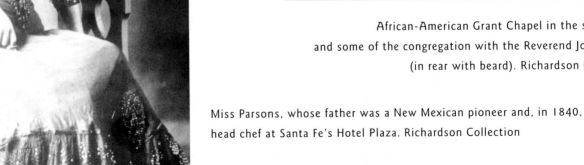

Miss Parsons, whose father was a New Mexican pioneer and, in 1840, head chef at Santa Fe's Hotel Plaza. Richardson Collection

and attended by the governor of Colorado and the mayor of Denver.

Their presence, however, was ignored when scholars, textbook writers, and movie and television scriptwriters spun their white frontier tales. Black women rarely appeared even as servants or cooks, maids or nannies.

It has been argued that

Children of pioneer Wesley McVey in Colorado. Standing: Hazel; in front: Helen, Kenneth, and Genevieve. Colorado Historical Society

since African-American women were a tiny minority within a western minority, omitting them was hardly an act of discrimination. Although few in number, they earned an honored niche in the saga of the wilderness. As the nation grapples with the history of its multicultural past, the story of frontier African-American women deserves a telling.

PIONEERS OF THE SLAVE ERA

This antique French print, "America," captured the racial mixture of Africans and Native Americans on the frontier. Bibliothèque Nationale, Paris, France

CHAPTER I

LIBERTY AMONG
THE INDIANS

By the time of the American Revolution, thousands of African-American slaves had escaped to find a refuge among Native American nations from Canada to Florida. The native people, not weighted down with color prejudice, offered the fugitives a hand of friendship. The sparsely settled frontier was a new chance to succeed for white people; for countless runaway slaves it meant freedom.

Hundreds, perhaps thousands, fled from the Carolinas and Georgia into the Spanish-claimed territory of Florida to become pioneer explorers there. Along the Appalachicola river, they were families of farmers, herders, and traders. In alliance with the Native Seminole nation they fought the United States to a standstill for forty-two years before the Civil War. Although most Seminoles, including black members of the group, finally became a part of the government's forced removal of Indians to the West, a small number did remain in Florida.

Photographed in the 20th century in Florida's Everglades, ancestors of the Seminoles once ruled the Florida Peninsula. William Loren Katz Collection

Choctaws of two races. William Loren Katz Collection

Some sixty-thousand Native Americans were forced from their homes in the southeastern states by Federal troops and driven westward to Oklahoma on what was called the Trail of Tears. Thousands of black women, men, children, Cherokees, Choctaws, Chickasaws, Creeks, and Seminoles trudged westward. In Oklahoma people of African descent accounted for 18 percent of the Cherokees, 14 percent of the Choctaws, 18 percent of the Chickasaws and 10 percent of the Creeks. Except among the Seminoles, most were slaves of Native American owners. Southern slaveholders had introduced African slaves to these "Five Civilized Nations" in an effort to keep them from offering a haven to escaped slaves of white slaveholders. Whites also believed that ownership of slaves could serve as an effort "to civilize" Indians.

But Native American slave practices differed markedly from that of southern whites. Indians permitted their slaves to remain in family groups and to eat with and intermarry with their masters. Still, all was not peaceful. In Oklahoma in 1842, 60 to 250 African-American men and women revolted and defeated their Cherokee owners in a two-day battle. Fresh Cherokee troops arrived and captured the rebels on an open prairie.

In 1860, a Native-American census in Oklahoma listed these slave members: Cherokees, 2,511; Choctaws, 2,344; Creeks, 1,532; and Chickasaws, 975.

In 1860 near Carson City, Nevada, an African-American man who had been running gunpowder and Bowie knives to the Indians for a year was seized by a posse. A newspaper reported, "He has an Indian squaw and lives with them." It

These Choctaws appeared in 1899 to claim their share of a U.S. distribution of funds to the Indian nations in Oklahoma. University of Oklahoma Library

A Cherokee mother and her daughter, who reflect a mixture that includes people of African descent. William Loren Katz Collection

also reported that he escaped. He was one of only forty-four people of color in Nevada then and ten of them were women. But he was one of thousands of African-American men during the years of slavery who married Native American women. A significant motivation for such marriages was that children born of a slave father and a free woman could not be enslaved.

After the Civil War, many men and women who shared this biracial heritage remained in the Oklahoma territory with their Native American nations. Other African Americans went west to seek their American dream as members of Indian nations.

In 1893 after a visit to the Flathead nation in Montana, the noted Army Chaplain Theophilis Steward wrote: "Among the Flatheads is a young African woman fully Indianized, speaking the language of the Indians and wearing their dress."

In 1942, researcher Kenneth W. Porter visited members of the black Seminole nation in Brackettville, Texas and

These descendants of African Seminoles were photographed by scholar Kenneth Wiggins Porter during World War II. William Loren Katz Collection

Nacimiento, Mexico. He discovered that many, but not all, were poor. The women were the ones who supplied the most reliable information. Rebecca Wilson, he wrote, "operates an excellent cafe, owns an attractive home and a large car, and has sent a couple of daughters to college." Rosa Fay, in her eighties and a most perceptive keeper of the Seminole flame, was particularly "clear and informative" and showed an ability to use "the striking and vigorous phrase." He continued: "Although in her eighties, she was as vigorous as a well-preserved woman in her early sixties, displaying tremendous strength and energy in her care of her hopelessly paralyzed and bed-ridden son."

A THIRST FOR FREEDOM

The seizure of men and women by slave catchers had an impact on entire families, and led fugitives to think of heading westward. William Loren Katz Collection

The Northwest Ordinance, passed by the Continental Congress in 1787, prohibited slavery in the region north of the Ohio River. Some slaveholders, determined to bring their slaves to the Ohio Valley, ignored the law. Others circumvented it by claiming their slaves were long-term apprentices or lifetime indentured servants.

Slavery in the Ohio Valley was finally defeated not by the law but by community action. Large numbers of northern whites who vigorously opposed slavery settled the region. And slave men and women managed to mount their own resistance.

Beginning in the 1830s, African-American women filed petitions demanding the Ordinance prohibiting slavery be enforced on masters and false apprenticeship be stopped. Scholar Darlene Clark Hine wrote: "One of the connecting threads in the history of Black women in the Northwest is the relentless quest for freedom and for equal enjoyment of educational, social and economic opportunities."

In the earliest case, *Boon v. Juliet,* in 1836 in Illinois, slave owner Bennington Boon, though his indenture of slave Juliet had expired, claimed he still owned her three children. With white anti-slavery friends assisting her, Juliet began a legal suit for her children and the court ruled in her favor.

Nothing could keep Thornton and Ruth Blackburn from finding each other and freedom. In 1833, two years after the couple escaped to Detroit, Kentucky, slaveholders had

This Brady Civil War photograph shows a slave family that escaped to the Union lines. Some families headed West after reaching freedom. William Loren Katz Collection

them jailed. During Sunday visiting hours, however, Ruth Blackburn exchanged clothes with Mrs. George French, walked out, and fled to Canada. On Monday dozens of armed African Americans rescued Thornton from the sheriff, and he joined his wife in Canada. After defeating a Canadian arrest effort, the couple became wealthy citizens of Toronto.

During the 1850s in Keokuk, Iowa, Charlotta Pyles opened her home as a station on the underground railroad. An activist, she also collected funds to buy the freedom of her relatives still held as slaves. She was aided by white abolitionists. Pyles began a speaking tour of eastern states to raise funds for the purchase of relatives still in bondage.

In Minnesota, a free state, women slaves used the law to try to free themselves. Rachael was a slave who was taken by her master to several army posts between 1831 and 1834. Once she

Black families reunited in 1865 in frontier Arkansas as soldiers are discharged from the U. S. Army. *Harper's Weekly*, William Loren Katz Collection

touched free land in Minnesota, she insisted, she was entitled to her liberty. In 1835, her case reached the Minnesota Supreme Court, but she was not freed. But Eliza Winston, a slave brought to the state in 1860 by her master, found abolitionists who helped her gain her liberty.

Once liberated, African Americans then tried to free their families. "Black Ann" was a highly praised cook on a Mississippi steamboat who earned enough money to purchase her children from their owner. Jane Snowden Thomas, an former slave from Missouri, in 1852 bought her son Billy, eleven, for $500 and mother and son journeyed to Oregon.

The opening of the Oregon Trail meant that the black drive for liberty pushed ever westward. In 1844, slaves Robin and Polly Holmes were brought by their owner to Oregon. He promised to emancipate the family after they helped him start a farm. The farm completed, he freed the couple but still insisted on holding the three Holmes children as slaves. In 1852, the couple brought suit for their children, a judge decided in their favor, and the family was reunited.

CHAPTER 3

BUILDING IN THE WILDERNESS

By the early nineteenth century, free African-American women and men resided on every frontier. Some had begun as slaves, had been freed by their owners, and had headed toward the freedom offered by the wilderness. Others escaped their chains to seek a home in lands far from slaveholders.

One of the earliest known settlements of free African Americans began in 1832 when 385 men, women, and children reached Mercer County, Ohio. These former Virginia slaves, freed in the will of politician John Randolph of Roanoke, traveled by wagon and boat. The will also provided them transportation and two to four thousand acres of fertile Ohio farmland. When they arrived, the former slaves found they had been cheated out of

Unidentified African-American pioneer family outside their wooden cabin, some members dressed in their Sunday best. William Loren Katz Collection

Sarah Jane Woodson was the first black woman graduate of Oberlin College to become a teacher. Oberlin College Archives

Oberlin College in Ohio began admitting African Americans and women in 1833. The first black Oberlin graduate to become a teacher was Sarah Jane Woodson. She was born in 1825 in Ohio, the youngest of eleven children. The Woodsons and other African-American families migrated from Virginia to Ohio in 1820 and formed a colony at Berlin in Jackson County. Though men led community and religious enterprises, women made sure matters were completed.

Sarah Jane Woodson enrolled at Oberlin in 1852 and earned tuition money during vacations by teaching children in segregated schools in Circleville and Portsmouth, Ohio. She graduated in 1856 and taught at Ohio's Wilberforce College, one of the first of her race or sex accepted on a university faculty.

Pioneer men and women of color faced legal color bars everywhere. Territorial and state legislatures passed "Black Laws" that denied them the right to vote, serve in the militia or on juries, hold public office, or testify in court. Some states made it a criminal offense for anyone to bring in or employ a black woman or man from another state.

In order to stem the flow of African-American migrants, white territorial and state legislators voted on the imposition of steep entrance fees. In 1829, the Illinois legislature raised the entrance fee for a black migrant from $500 to $1,000, but the provision remained largely unenforced.

In the 1840s, across the river from St. Louis, African-American men and women founded Brooklyn, Illinois. In 1850, McLean County, Illinois had several African-

their land by Randolph's relatives. But white citizens of Piqua, Ohio held a meeting and voted to feed and provide work for the pioneers.

That same year another colony of African Americans, many with Cherokee blood, left Northampton, North Carolina to start the Roberts Settlement in Hamilton County, Indiana. They built log cabins, a church, and a school. Their community soon produced farmers, teachers, ministers, and, during the Civil War, soldiers and nurses for the Union army.

American residents, including a twenty-year-old school-teacher born in Kentucky. In 1850, a frontier Missouri county listed sixteen people of color, including five women.

It became a criminal offense in Indiana in 1851 for any person to encourage an African American to enter or "remain in the state." Those who violated the law were fined from $10 to $500. In 1854, this Indiana law ended the marriage of two young African-American pioneers. Elizabeth Keith, a resident of Ohio, and Arthur Barkshire, who had lived in Rising Sun, Indiana for ten years, were married in Indiana. Barkshire was found guilty of "harboring" Keith. He was fined $10, and their marriage was nullified. The Barkshires appealed to the Indiana Supreme Court, but it upheld the Black Laws.

A constitutional policy so decisively adopted, and so clearly conducive to the separation and ultimate good of both races, should be rigidly enforced. [Barkshire] can claim nothing from the supposed relation of husband and wife . . . [and] can, therefore, be regarded only as any other person would be who encouraged the negro woman Elizabeth to remain in the state.

The judges also said that Elizabeth Keith could be arrested "for coming into the state or settling here."

To combat Black Laws, discriminatory customs, and white violence, people of color organized protest conventions and sent delegates to national black conventions. In the 1840s and 1850s, black people in Ohio held seven statewide conventions, six in Columbus and one in Cincinnati. Women supported the conventions, but only men were listed as official delegates.

To build community and to unite behind issues dear to them, African-American women formed self-help clubs in western territories and states. In Detroit, Chicago, and Cleveland, early societies focused on aid to the elderly and the poor, and ill and orphaned children. For example, in 1843 in Detroit, women formed what would later be called The Colored Ladies Benevolent Society.

Despite laws and unrelenting white resentment, people of color continued to settle the frontier. In 1857, when Minneapolis was still called St. Anthony, Emily Grey was part of the town's African-American community. The next year, the year Minnesota became a state, Grey began to convert a barn into a spacious home. Packing boxes covered with calico became her bureaus and cupboards. She became active on public issues, urging her community to improve its health-care program, take better care of its poor, and upgrade the inferior education it offered children of color.

In 1860, the census reports for a dozen western states and territories showed the 50 percent school attendance for black women equaled that of white women. The 26 percent illiteracy rate for African-American women on the frontier was much lower than for white frontier women. Women of color in the wilderness consistently distinguished themselves through their dedication to self-improvement and zeal for education.

THE ORDEAL OF
DRED AND HARRIET SCOTT

For ten years and ten months the Scott family—Dred Scott, Harriet, and their two daughters, Lizzie and Eliza—battled the United States for their freedom.

In the early 1830s, Dr. John Emerson, Scott's owner, was sent to Fort Armstrong, Illinois. He took Scott with him into the Ohio Valley. Then, in 1836, Emerson took Scott to Fort Snelling, Minnesota. There, Emerson purchased a slave woman named Harriet, whom Scott married. In 1839, the Scotts had a daughter Eliza, born on a Mississippi riverboat, the *Gypsy*. The Missouri Compromise of 1820 had banned slavery in Minnesota and other northern territories. Eliza's birth was in free territory north of the Missouri Compromise line.

Dr. Emerson and the Scott family returned to Jefferson Barracks, Missouri, where Harriet Scott gave birth to another daughter, Lizzie. In 1843, Dr. Emerson died, leaving the Scott family to his wife. Mrs. Emerson hired Scott out to work for others. By 1846, Scott had returned to St. Louis and offered to purchase his liberty and that of his family with $300 he had saved from doing odd jobs. Mrs. Emerson turned down his offer but the Scott family had decided they wanted to be free.

For ten years Dred Scott fought in the courts for the freedom of his family.
William Loren Katz Collection

She sold the Scott family to John Sanford of New York. By this time, Dred Scott was called "dissatisfied with this treatment" and "resolved to sue in court for liberty." His legal brief said Scott had resided in territories where slavery had been banned by the Northwest Ordinance or a law of Congress. In 1847, Dred Scott, representing his family, took his action before a circuit court judge in the east wing of the old St. Louis courthouse. In the second count of his petition, Scott sued for his wife Harriet, and in the third he sued for his children, Eliza, fourteen, and Lizzie, seven.

The Scotts were represented by two white attorneys who charged the Scott family had been victims of assault and false imprisonment. They asked for damages of $10. When they lost their first trial, the Scotts moved for a new trial, which was granted in December 1847.

Harriet Scott, whose perseverance finally led to freedom for her family. William Loren Katz Collection

In January 1850, a judge granted them liberty, since the family had touched free land. But the government appealed the ruling and it was reversed. In 1852, the family sued again and lost. Next the Scotts pursued their case to the Supreme Court on "a writ of error." By this time, donations from white abolitionists were helping Scott pay legal fees. Abolitionists hoped for a high court decision that would ban slavery's expansion to the West, and in that way seal its doom.

President-elect James Buchanan decided to enter the case on the pro-slavery side, even if it meant violating the "separation of powers" provision of the Constitution. He secretly wrote a letter to Justice John Catron opposing Scott's petition, and his views were speedily conveyed to Justices Robert Grier, James Wayne, and Chief Justice Roger Taney. Catron then wrote to Buchanan of "their concurrence."

In his 1857 inaugural address, President Buchanan called on his fellow Americans to submit to the forthcoming Supreme Court decision. He gave no hint that he had conspired to defeat the Scotts's bid for liberty and had violated the Constitution. The Supreme Court ruled that the Scotts and other people of color had no right to bring a case to a federal court. Justice Taney's decision said people of color had no rights that whites were bound to respect.

By then, however, Dred and Harriet Scott had been purchased by a new owner, Taylor Blow, who soon freed them. They settled in St. Louis. Dred became a hotel porter, Harriet ran a laundry. They were finally free and happy.

FRONTIER AGITATORS

Sojourner Truth.
William Loren Katz
Collection

As a voice raised against human bondage and for women's rights, Sojourner Truth, a tall, gaunt, former New York slave, had few peers. Her public impact was not diminished by the fact that she could not read or write. After years as an agitator in eastern states, in 1851 Sojourner Truth claimed God asked her to "go West." Setting out for Ohio to attend an anti-slavery convention, she spoke to large, rapt audiences along the way. During the next decade she carried her campaign into the midwest.

Truth faced shouting pro-slavery crowds in the midwest, and once ended up hoarse trying to yell over their jeers. On one occasion, an angry crowd forced her to leave the meeting. Another time, a sheriff arrested her to protect her from a mob. When she was told a gang planned to burn down her meeting hall, she said, "I'll speak on the ashes."

In the 1850s, Truth carried her anti-slavery campaign through Indiana and Ohio riding in a borrowed horse and buggy. Her sign read: "Proclaim liberty throughout all the land unto all the inhabitants thereof" and her wagon carried six hundred copies of her autobiography. Her aim was to "abolitionize" states across the Ohio River from the slave states of Kentucky and Virginia, persuading people in these free states to aid escaping slaves.

At one meeting Sojourner Truth scoffed at a lawyer who said people of color were innately inferior. Another man challenged her by saying, "Why I don't care any more for your talk than I do for the bite of a flea." She answered, "Lord willing I'll keep you scratchin'."

In 1857 Truth, then sixty, ended her midwest tour and moved to Harmonia, Michigan, near Battle Creek. The town had fifty-four other African Americans and a white mayor who served as a conductor on the underground railroad. From her new home, she repeatedly urged African Americans to "go West" and begin life anew in a free land.

Many black and white women became involved in the anti-slavery crusade and campaigns to remove western Black Laws that denied people of color the right to vote, hold office, or testify in court. Scholar Herbert Aptheker reported that in the 1830s, women's anti-slavery organizations with black and white members and leaders "proliferated within a few years . . . into the Midwest, Ohio, Illinois, and Michigan particularly."

Black men and women in Troy, Michigan in 1836 formed an auxiliary to the American Anti-Slavery Society. And after white American women declared their rights at a convention in 1848 in Seneca Falls, black conventions "generally seated women, although the delegates sometimes needed prodding. Women themselves were not loathe to

force the issue." At the Ohio state convention in 1849, women "threatened a boycott," writes scholar Benjamin Quarles.

Wives of several prominent western abolitionists and civil rights leaders played their role, most often behind the scenes. In March 1829, free black John Malvin married Harriet Dorsey and the couple moved to Louisville, then to Middletown, Kentucky so they could be near his wife's father, Caleb Dorsey. The couple decided to leave the state after an incident in which Malvin was arrested as a fugitive slave, handcuffed, and badly beaten.

Malvin purchased a small farm for his wife and himself in Canada and in 1831 they left for Canada. By the time they reached Buffalo, New York, Harriet decided she could not leave her enslaved father behind. "It lay so heavily upon her that she gave me no rest. Seeing her unwillingness to go to Canada, and her fears that she would never see her father again, I concluded to give up the farm, and my wife having taken a fancy to Cleveland, was determined to go back and settle there."

With the $100 down payment in savings and promissory notes raised from friends, and over her husband's objections, Mrs. Malvin journeyed to Kentucky alone to buy her father's freedom. At a time when women did not travel by themselves or engage in financial arrangements, she negotiated her sixty-year-old father's manumission and brought him back to Cleveland.

John and Harriet Malvin spent the rest of their lives battling for racial justice in Ohio. The couple organized a First

Baptist Church in Cleveland and in 1835 they helped erect its first building on Seneca and Champlain Streets, where John Malvin occasionally addressed the mostly white congregation. Then, shocked to find the church had instituted a special, isolated "Nigger Pew" for black church members, the Malvins fought this insult and injustice. When they alone were offered a choice of seats, the couple rejected this compromise and opposed the church's segregation policy for another eighteen months. They finally won a reversal that eliminated any discrimination.

In 1841 in Memphis, Tennessee free people of color John Jones and Mary Richardson, daughter of a black-smith, married. For the next four years they were active abolitionists who secretly aided slave runaways. In 1845, with $3.50 they had saved, the couple moved to free Illinois. There, they had a daughter, Lavinia, and began to expand their anti-slavery activities. Their home became a station on the underground railroad. One day a detective friend and abolitionist, Allan Pinkerton, brought a man named John Brown to the house. The Joneses contributed money to help finance his famous raid on Harpers Ferry. The couple also denounced the state's Black Laws in a pamphlet written by John Jones. In 1875, the Jones family publicly celebrated thirty years in Chicago fighting for liberty and justice.

Mrs. Mary Richardson Jones and her husband were active abolitionists in Illinois, where their home was a station on the underground railroad. William Loren Katz Collection

CONFLICT IN CALIFORNIA

The Native Americans of California who did not die at the hands of the Spanish conquistadors intermixed with Europeans and Africans, free and former slaves, who emigrated there. This process continued as Mexico wrenched free of Spanish control in the 1820s. In 1829, President Vicente Guerrero, a black Indian and a former revolutionary leader, abolished slavery in Mexico.

In a 1790 Census, African-American men and women constituted 18 percent of California's population. Los Angeles was founded in 1781 by forty-four people, twenty-six of them of African descent. Maria

Pio Pico, whose grandmother was listed in Spain's 1790 census of California as a person of mixed African, Indian, and Spanish blood, grew up to become the last Governor of Mexico's California before the Americans took over. He is shown here with his wife. William Loren Katz Collection

Miss Helen Warner in her stenography office in 1904 in Los Angeles, California. She represented a rising educated black middle class that had its origins in the Gold Rush. William Loren Katz Collection

Rita Valdez, born to one of these African families in Los Angeles, owned what is now Beverly Hills.

In 1848, the treaty that ended the Mexican War awarded California to the United States. The discovery of gold in 1849 brought a rush of fortune seekers that included thousands of slave owners and their slaves.

A slave named "Mary," brought by her owner from Missouri in 1846, may have been the first of her race to reach California from the East. She *was* the first person of African descent to sue for her liberty in the West. Perhaps she was moved to action when she found out that Mexican law had ended slavery. In a San Jose court, Mary asked for her freedom, and a justice of the peace ruled in her favor.

In 1852, the two thousand African Americans in California amounted to 1 percent of the state's population. By 1860, the census counted 2,827 African-American men and 1,259 women. Most black women and men chose to live in cities, working at occupations other than gold mining. But some returned to the East with glowing tales of gold strikes. In Genevieve City, Missouri, Mrs. Alley Brown heard from her husband laboring in California's Cosumne diggings: "This is the best place for black folks on the globe. All a man has to do is to work and he will make money."

Gold Rush California became the wealthiest African-American area in the country. Rising black expectations led to demands for education, civil rights, and other reforms. In 1853, a number of prominent figures opened the San Francisco Atheneum as a cultural center. It had a saloon on the first floor, but the Atheneum's pride was its second floor. There, in a year, sponsors raised $2,000 to create an eight-hundred-book library and a museum that served as a hub of black intellectual life.

During the 1850s, Elizabeth Thorn Scott opened the first African-American schools in Sacramento and later Oakland. Other African-American women teachers founded schools in San Francisco, Sacramento, and Red Bluff.

In Sacramento, in 1859, African-American parents began their own school for thirty to thirty-five pupils, mostly girls, and hired a white teacher. Within a year the city Board of Education awarded three of its female pupils silver achievement medals.

But in 1858, Sarah Lester, fifteen, the light-skinned daughter of a wealthy bootmaker and civil rights activist family, had graduated from San Francisco's white Spring Valley school. She entered a white high school and scored second highest in academic achievement and first in art and music.

Suddenly a local paper demanded she be expelled and debate roiled the city. Though white fellow students threatened a school boycott if their popular classmate was removed, the school board finally ordered Sarah Lester's expulsion. The Lesters, father, mother, and daughter, left for Canada where Sarah wrote a friend, "I can scarcely bear to talk about schools."

BIDDY MASON

Biddy Mason, born in Hancock County, Georgia, was a lowly slave destined for a dramatic life and great wealth in California. As a slave, owned by Robert Marion Smith of Mississippi, she had three children—Ellen, born in 1838, Ann, born in 1844, and Harriet, born in 1848.

After Smith became a Mormon convert, he decided to move his family closer to Salt Lake City. He started the journey in 1848 with fifty-six other whites, thirty-four slaves, seven milk cows, two yoke of oxen, eight mules, and dozens of wagons. Biddy Mason demonstrated skill and endurance on the trail. She prepared meals, cared for her

Nancy Davis Lester, mother of Sarah Lester, fought to keep her daughter in an integrated California school in the 1850s. British Columbia Archives

children, and acted as midwife for others in the party. In September 1851, Smith decided to leave Nevada and head his wagons to San Bernardino, California. By then, Biddy Mason had walked most of the 2,000 miles from Georgia.

Smith then realized that his slaves might seek their liberty in California so he planned to take them back to a southern state and sell them. But the Masons had their own ideas. One of Biddy Mason's daughters and another slave owned by Smith had become romantically involved with two free young black men, Charles Owens and Manuel Pepper. These men also did not want them to leave. When they learned of the Masons's plight, they brought a sheriff and legal papers to the Smith camp in the Santa Monica Mountains and Mrs. Mason served Robert Smith with a court order requiring him to prove these were his slaves before a judge.

Smith failed to appear in court to answer Mason's petition and after two days of hearings, Biddy Mason and her family were freed. Mason became a skilled nurse and midwife to wealthy Californians, and made extra money dealing in herbs and roots. Ten years after gaining her freedom, she paid $250 for a house on Spring Street in downtown Los Angeles. She was one of the first women of color to own a home under American rule.

Mason also began trading in real estate and as Los Angeles began to grow she built homes to rent out. Her grandson, Robert, a successful developer was, by the end of the century, the city's richest African American.

Biddy Mason became a noted philanthropist. She opened her home to the poor of every race and brought food to those held in the city's dank jail cells. In 1872, she helped found the First African Methodist Episcopal Church of Los Angeles. During a flood in the 1880s, she donated her own funds to establish free credit for homeless families at a neighborhood grocer.

On Palm Sunday, March 27, 1988, Mayor Tom Bradley, the first elected black mayor of the city, was among 3,000 people in Los Angeles who paid homage to Biddy Mason. A large tombstone was unveiled at her grave that celebrated her contribution to the city. In November 1989, with two of her great-granddaughters in attendance, many citizens celebrated Biddy Mason Day.

California pioneer and philanthropist Biddy Mason. William Loren Katz Collection

MARY PLEASANT

Mary Ellen Pleasant was photographed at the age of 87.
William Loren Katz Collection

Much about Mary Pleasant, a free woman of color, still remains a mystery. No one knows when she left the East for California, but in the East she was said to have donated money to John Brown for his raid on Harpers Ferry.

In California, Mary Pleasant was known for her daring and determination. She rode off in her wagon to rescue slaves in rural areas. Some say she ran a station on the underground railroad. As a businesswoman, she helped build the Atheneum as a cultural center and invested in the saloon on the first floor.

During the Civil War, Mary Pleasant was active in the struggle to gain full civil rights for her people. She went before a California court and won the right of people of color to testify in cases involving whites. In 1866 she personally challenged a San Francisco streetcar company's policy of segregation in court and won a $600 judgment.

Some scholars, however, have seen another side to Mary Pleasant's impressive victories for humanity, and say she had a shady personal life as a money lender and a bordello owner who catered to the state's wealthiest men. Some historians have called her a financial meddler, a con artist, and a "crafty survivor." She was successful at business, that much is sure, and in the long fight to win equal rights for African Americans in California. The full truth may never be known about the extraordinary woman named Mary Pleasant.

CHAPTER 7

CLARA BROWN OF COLORADO

Clara Brown was a hearty pioneer woman whose spirituality deeply affected everyone she met. Though she grew into a tall, attractive young woman, her mother told her, she wrote, "pretty is as pretty does, and I was early taught not to go much on the good looks. They thought more of good behavior and politeness than they does now."

Born into slavery in Kentucky, Clara Brown knew the sorrow of separation from her family. Her husband Richard, her son Richard, Jr., and her daughters Margaret, Palina Ann, and Eliza Jane were all sold as slaves to different owners. Of her tragedies, Brown said, "the Lord He give me strength to bear up under them." Religious faith would sustain and energize her.

In 1856, her master George Brown died and his will freed Clara Brown and left her some money. But Kentucky law required that emancipated slaves leave the state, so Brown traveled to Fort Leavenworth, Kansas. There, in 1859, people were joining together to travel to Pike's Peak, between Denver and Colorado Springs, Colorado, where gold had been discovered. Brown talked some prospectors into taking her along with them if she would do the cooking and washing. She loaded her pots and pans into their covered wagon and began the eight-week trip to Denver and the eastern slopes of the Rockies.

In 1859 when Brown reached Denver it was still called Cherry Creek. Colorado was two years away from a territorial government, and statehood lay sixteen years in the future.

After her arrival in Cherry Creek, Brown worked for a baker and found the time to help two Methodist ministers establish the Union Sunday School. In 1861 she moved to nearby Central City and bought a miner's cabin, which she turned into a laundry. She charged fifty cents for flannel shirts and business was booming. She also helped to nurse the sick.

Her house in Central City became the first home of the Methodist church. She also donated her labor and some money to build the first Protestant church building in the Rocky Mountains and donated money for a Catholic church as well.

Brown turned her home, reported a local paper, "into a hospital, a hotel and a general refuge for those who were sick or in poverty" including hungry Native Americans. "I go always where Jesus calls me, honey," she said.

When she expanded her laundry business and took in a partner, profits soared. She invested in real estate and by 1864 owned seven houses in Central City, sixteen lots in Denver, and property in Georgetown and Boulder.

Brown was ready for her life's goal—to reunite her family. In October 1865, with the Civil War over, trusting in God, she set out for Gallitan, Kentucky. She failed to find her own family, but returned with twenty-six former slaves—men, women, children, infants, and some orphans. She paid for their rail transportation to Leavenworth and then for the wagons that carried them to Denver. She also helped each find a home, a job, and an education.

She offered a $1,000 reward for information about her daughter, Eliza Jane, but heard nothing.

At age eighty Clara Brown was poor again. Efforts to locate her family and her charity to others had drained her re-

The only known photograph of Clara Brown.
William Loren Katz Collection

sources. She also found she had been cheated by real estate agents. Then in 1882, a former Denver friend wrote to say she had met Brown's daughter, Eliza Jane, who was then a fifty-year-old widow with the last name Brewer, living in Iowa.

With money borrowed from neighbors, Clara Brown bought a train ticket to Council Bluffs, Iowa. Eliza Jane was waiting for her. It was raining heavily and as the two women rushed to embrace at the railroad station, they slipped and fell in the mud. Water and mud did not dampen their joy. Mother and daughter returned to Denver to live. Together, they extended the Brown hospitality and aided more people in Colorado.

When Clara Brown was eighty-one, the Colorado Pioneers Association altered its rules to vote her its first woman member. And when Brown died in 1885, the Association arranged her funeral at the Central Presbyterian church. Her daughter, brother, granddaughter, and nieces attended. The eulogy was delivered by her minister and friend of seventeen years, Reverend E. P. Wells. He exhorted the mourners, who included the mayor of Denver and the Governor of Colorado, to emulate "one of the most unselfish lives on record," and "to reflect on her unexampled benevolence."

Later, a plaque was placed in the St. James Methodist Church to celebrate Brown's founding of this church in her home. A chair in the Denver Opera House acknowledged her contributions to Colorado. Clara Brown's life had served as a model of benevolence for thousands.

WESTWARD TO FREEDOM

Top left: Cherokee Bill and his mother, Ellen Lynch, who allegedly smuggled a revolver into his jail cell, leading to his last shootout, his last killing, and his execution in 1896. Fort Smith National Historic Site

Below left: Early notice of cheap land in Kansas for African Americans by promoter Benjamin "Pap" Singleton. William Loren Katz Collection

Top right: Born of African and Indian descent, Mamie Conners brought up a large family on her southwestern homestead. Richardson Collection

Below right: A Washington, Iowa, picnic.
William Loren Katz Collection

Ho for Kansas!

Brethren, Friends, & Fellow Citizens:

I feel thankful to inform you that the

REAL ESTATE

AND

Homestead   Association,

Will Leave Here the

15th of April, 1878,

In pursuit of Homes in the Southwestern Lands of America, at Transportation Rates, cheaper than ever was known before.

For full information inquire of

Benj. Singleton, better known as old Pap,

NO. 5 NORTH FRONT STREET.

Beware of Speculators and Adventurers, as it is a dangerous thing to fall in their hands.

Nashville, Tenn., March 18, 1878.

THE WAGONS OF OPPORTUNITY

The turmoil of the Civil War allowed hundreds of thousands of men and women to escape from slave states. A small number fled to the frontier seeking a new life. In Missouri, Howard C. Bruce and his fiancée did not wait for legal emancipation to reach the state. They armed themselves and secretly made their way to the frontier. On March 31, 1864, they reached Fort Leavenworth, Kansas, put aside their weapons, and were married by Reverend John Turner of the African Methodist Episcopal Church.

With emancipation and the war's end, African Americans could reach the frontier without fear of being followed, seized, and returned to slavery. In 1865, Nancy Lewis, an attractive, vivacious teenager also traveled to Fort Leavenworth where she met and soon married a former Union veteran. To build a new life for themselves, the young couple joined a wagon train as it bumped its way across the

A soldier's wife in 1868, Mrs. Howard (left) stayed on to raise her family in the southwest. Richardson Collection

prairie to Denver, Colorado. In 1945, Lewis, spry as ever at ninety-eight, was satisfied with her life's choices. But she shared a regret with many frontier women: "I can't read or write, and it's my own fault." Nancy Lewis's illiteracy, though, put her in a minority among African-American women on the frontier, who had a much higher rate of literacy than their white counterparts.

African-American women who went West after the war were unusual in other ways, too. First, they were largely in their twenties to forties, older than average white pioneer

Sally and George Davis, pioneers.
William Loren Katz Collection

Kate Rose and her adopted son.
Before she died at 106, Rose had
become a renowned cook and had
founded a church in the southwest.
Richardson Collection

women. Second, they were more likely to be married than white women. Third, being closer to the end of their childbearing years, they had a much lower childbearing rate than white women. Compared to their southern sisters, they produced half the number of children per family.

Unlike white pioneers, most former slave women (and men) rejected farm work for town jobs. They associated rural life with the pain and social isolation of southern plantations and slavery. (During this time, European peasant immigrants, for similar reasons, overwhelmingly chose urban life over rural life in America. They associated farm work with the oppressive conditions they had fled in Europe.)

For a white woman, a job on the frontier usually served as a bridge between arrival time and marriage. For a woman of color, married or unmarried, a paying job was a necessity. Black women of the West were five times as likely to be employed as white women and twice as likely to be employed as Asian or Native American women.

Black women in cities were often domestic servants. They found their new salaries often double or triple the pay in the East. Those who settled in towns had an even lower childbearing rate than women in rural settings. And the larger the town, the fewer children per family. This indicates a focus on career, small family, education for children, and other middle-class goals.

For most women, the West expanded opportunities, led to wider choices, and lifted some conventional restrictions imposed in the East. Women of color also gained

Tall, stately Luticia Parsons in 1870. She was a nurse for the Buffalo Soldiers in the southwest.
Richardson Collection

from the breakdown of traditional gender work roles in the West, though less than white women. In the West they found racial barriers such as those they faced in the East were far fewer or enforced less often. In the West they faced far less racial anger and violence.

Women of any color were scarce on the frontier. Their relative rarity in western communities gave them a wide choice of suitors and more opportunities to marry. The marriage rate for western women of color soared ahead of their sisters in other parts of the country. Black men, drawn to western towns by jobs, might outnumber black women by more than ten to one. In many towns eager black men were said to meet incoming trains and stagecoaches hoping to find their marriage partners.

In the 1890s Mary Lewis ran Tucson, Arizona's Alhambra Cafeteria. Richardson Collection

Martha Williams helped care for Arizona and New Mexico orphans, and was the mother of Cathy Williams, who secretly served in the Buffalo Soldiers as a man. Richardson Collection

Right: New Mexico homesteader Kitty Wood, born in 1836 and mother of ten children. After being scalped at 33 by Indians, she wore a cap until her death at 103. Richardson Collection

Below: The Mount Pilgrim Baptist Church and congregation in Raton, New Mexico. Richardson Collection

CHAPTER 9

MAIL ORDER BRIDES OF THE SOUTHWEST

Mail order bride Grace Johnson. Richardson Collection

A highly unusual westward migration was carried out by mail order brides. In response to the scarcity of women on early frontiers, some young ladies in the East made an extraordinary decision. They agreed to leave home and family, promised to board frontier-bound trains, and marry the men who paid for their tickets. Marriage by mail order for young women became a brisk western business for white communities and for African-American communities as the nineteenth century turned into the twentieth century.

In Arizona mining camps, the idea was first proposed not by men but married African-American women. They found the presence of so many young men in their community unsettling. With too few women to go around, the wrong kind of women came to town, and fights among the men were frequent. The answer, they convinced unmarried men

In the early 20th century the Busy Bee Club
met to arrange for mail order brides for Arizona
miners. Richardson Collection

including many widowers, was an arranged marriage to a mail order bride.

To locate appropriate candidates, eastern churches and newspapers were put to use. Marriage-minded young ladies responded to the invitation. Each had to be willing to board a train for Arizona and to marry the working man who paid in advance for her one-way ticket.

Filled with hope, young candidates set out from Boston, Philadelphia, and New York. Many left lives of poverty, family problems, or personal tragedies. Each sought her American dream, a new beginning. They hoped to find the thrill of love, the warmth of family, and a new life.

Their trains raced through strange, unfamiliar lands. Each of the young women—and some were mere girls who had just entered their teen years—prepared for the shock of that first meeting in Arizona.

Some of the Arizona miners had lived through several wives. Frontier childbirths under less than sanitary conditions carried off many a young wife and mother. A husband

Mail order bride
Georgia Williams.
Richardson Collection

On their wedding day in Arizona, these young miners' brides appeared worried about their future out west and as wives. Richardson Collection

buried his wife and turned from his grief
to take care of a large family alone.
Miners in Arizona could not afford servants, and relatives were few. Soon widowers began to think about another
hand to help, another wife, another
mother for the children.

Before the trains rolled westward, the
men had met in Arizona to decide who
would select their partner first, second,
and third. An old American principle
won: seniority. The oldest men gained
the right to make the first choice.
Sometimes men old enough to be their fathers or grandfa-
thers selected the youngest candidates. As fathers, they
hoped that in this marriage youth, sturdy character, physical
endurance, and luck would promote successful families.
More than a few brides found they had inherited a house
full of children.

Wedding-day photographs of mail order brides show attractive young African-American women. Some photos
captured a bride's nervous smile or sad, worried eyes. Vul-
nerable young women, never before married and thousands
of miles from home and family, wondered about their new
lives as married women.

CHAPTER 10

FRONTIER WOMEN AND LIFE'S GOALS

More than a few western women of color found their fondest wishes fulfilled at the edge of the wilderness: in marriage, family, and sometimes landownership or success in business. Compared to their sisters back East, they were less likely to have suffered white rape, child abuse, or to have seen family members subjected to white assaults or police brutality. Families were likely to receive a decent education and better pay than back East. More than anywhere else in the United States at the time, the frontier offered African Americans a chance in life. Most were glad they made the trip.

By the last decades of the nineteenth century, the frontier was no longer a "man's domain." Women rose steadily as a percentage of the western African-American population. In Nevada in

The Speese family, Nebraska homesteaders, in 1888. William Loren Katz Collection

The Hannah family, homesteaders in Nebraska: Grace, Truth, Glenn, father Robert, and mother (name not given).
William Loren Katz Collection

1860, the African-American population was 77 percent male. By 1870, the figure for men was 67 percent and by 1880 it was 63 percent. Outnumbered by their men by almost four to one in Nevada before the Civil War, within a single generation in Nevada, women accounted for one of every three African Americans. By 1900, African-American women outnumbered their men in Los Angeles and Denver.

Census statistics show that African-American women on the frontier made a determined assault on their ignorance, which was the inheritance of slavery. In a generation or two, they overcame illiteracy. There may be no parallel in history to the massive, rapid march of families from the illiteracy forced on slaves to the education free people of color gained on the frontier.

Frontier women vigorously pursued education for their children, too, though it often meant great financial sacrifices. Over half the teenage African-American women attended school. Many families kept their daughters in school and sent their sons to work. Between 1890 and 1910, illiteracy among African-American women in western communities in some areas dropped to less than 10 percent.

Prompted by their eager parents, children were more likely than not to attend school. When allowed, they sat in classes with white children. When there was no other choice, parents accepted segregated schooling. The children had to be educated.

ELVIRA CONLEY

In 1864 Elvira Conley, a tall, statuesque, nineteen-year-old former slave left a failed marriage and headed west on her own. In 1868, she was one of 2,000 residents of Sheridan, Kansas, a rowdy frontier railroad town. Sheridan's good citizens finally appointed a Vigilante Committee to bring law and order to their lawless town.

Conley did her best to avoid trouble. She opened a laundry and cleaned the blue shirts of Buffalo Bill and Wild Bill Hickok, two of the West's best gunslingers. As a woman alone, her friendship with them may have shielded her from the town's outlaws.

The next year, when the John Bullard family left Sheridan to travel further west, they hired Conley as a governess. For her next sixty years and through three generations of Bullards and Sellars, she helped raise children. Awed and delighted children and grandchildren heard Conley's exciting tales of Buffalo Bill and Wild Bill Hickok.

Mrs. Barbara Storke had been brought up by Conley. In 1981 and in her seventies, Mrs. Storke recalled Elvira Conley as "an amazing and wonderful woman, born into slavery [who] carved out a life in what we now call 'the wild west.'" This was her vivid impression of her former governess: "She was black, black as ebony and she was proud of it. She knew who she was. The majesty of her bearing, her great pride always commanded respect."

Conley died in 1929 but those who had been touched by her gentle and awesome presence were still reminiscing about their beloved governess and friend at the end of the century.

Elvira Conley in early Kansas around 1869. William Loren Katz Collection

Elvira Conley with the Sellars-Bullard family around 1890, possibly in New Mexico. William Loren Katz Collection

CHAPTER II

EXODUS TO KANSAS

Families on the way to Kansas by riverboat. In May 1879, a *Harper's Weekly* artist sketched this scene at Vicksburg, Mississippi. William Loren Katz Collection

After the Civil War, the South's slave system was replaced by a sharecropper system. Whites forced African Americans to work for them as underpaid laborers. Jim Crow laws enacted after the Civil War denied African Americans rights to vote, hold office, gain an education, and opportunities for advancement. By the 1870s, violence against people of color rose in many southern states and it did not spare mothers, daughters, and children.

Black families began to discuss a future on a frontier free of racial hatred. In 1879, at least ten thousand African Americans left states in the deep South. Called the "Exodus of 1879," they were part of a desperate effort to find safety and land in

Kansas. One sharecropper wrote to Kansas Governor John P. St. John:

Some of us are almost naked and starved. . . . We have to keep our intentions secret or be shot; and we are not allowed to meet. . . . There are forty widows in our band. They are work-women and farmers also. The white men here take our wives and daughters, and serve them as they please, and we are shot if we say any thing about it; and if we vote any other way than their way we can not live in our State or county. We are sure to leave, or be killed.

Women were a driving force in the "Exodus of 1879." Black Louisiana state senator John Burch, testifying on the migration before a Congressional Committee, said "the women have had more to do with it than all the politics and the men."

Women indeed became among the earliest and most consistent emigration voices. At a New Orleans convention in

Exodusters who reached West Topeka, Kansas, in 1880 are welcomed by Governor St. John and his wife (at right near second barrel). William Loren Katz Collection

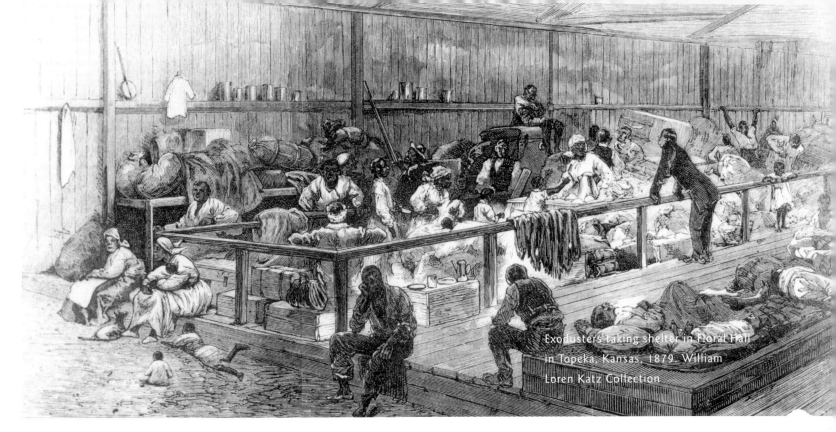

Exodusters taking shelter in Floral Hall in Topeka, Kansas, 1879. William Loren Katz Collection

1875, women delegates, many of them widows whose husbands had been slain by racists in Alabama, Mississippi, Georgia, and Texas, emerged as a decisive force in the flight to Kansas. Women began to serve as planners and grass roots leaders of the exodus.

Husbands and fathers felt helpless in the face of terror. "We can do nothing to protect the virtue of our wives and daughters," a father told Kansas relief worker Laura Haviland. Some wives said they would leave the South even if their husbands refused. Henry Adams of Louisiana, the movement's most influential figure, recalled a crucial vote for the exodus: "in a unanimous voice . . . echoed by all; and we all agreed to it, both men and women that were assembled at the conference." Perhaps for the first time in history men and women had democratically voted to launch a huge migration to save their lives.

By April 1879, thousands of families took riverboats up the Mississippi River or walked up the Chisolm Trail to Kansas. Landowners reacted with fury to losing their cheap labor. In May, armed whites closed the Mississippi to the "exodusters" and threatened to sink their boats. General Thomas Conway wired President Hayes that it looked "as if we are at war."

In Kansas in 1882, the Salisbury pioneer family posed for a family portrait in formal clothing. Richardson Collection

The Exodusters oured into Kansas in such numbers that relief facilities became strained. African American Josephine St. Pierre Ruffin headed the Kansas Relief Association, and Clara Brown arrived from Colorado to help with donations and offer her labor. They worked with white women, among them Laura S. Haviland, to raise money, collect food and clothing, and try to find jobs and homes for the exodusters.

From September 1879 to May 1881, Haviland reported the Kansas Relief Association spent over $90,000 in contributions, including $13,000 from English Quakers, with donations of clothing, thousands of blankets, scissors, spoons, and needles. Within a year, families settled down and needed little help. Haviland wrote:

Comparatively few [exodusters] call for assistance who have been in the State a year, and most of these are aged grandparents, the sick, and widows with large families of small children.

Of those who came in the early Spring of 1879, many have raised from one hundred to four hundred bushels of corn each year, but divide with their friends and relatives who follow them.

By 1880, African-American women were 4.6 percent of the Kansas population, a higher percentage than any other western state. A symbol of the African-American presence was eleven chapters of the First Grand Benevolent Society of Kansas and Missouri, an organization founded by African-American women to care for members in sickness, poverty, and adversity.

Another sign of the African-American presence in Kansas was the 160-acre town of Nicodemus founded in 1877 by six African Americans and one white man. By 1878, Nicodemus had 600 inhabitants, almost all African American, and was the most populous town north of the Kansas Pacific Railroad tracks and west of Beloit. To plant their crops, determined settlers turned the land by hand using spades and hoes. Some hitched their milk cows to plows.

Nicodemus's citizens focused their attention on education. Their first school, begun in 1879, operated in the sod home of its instructor, Mrs. Francis Fletcher. Her fifteen pupils sat on big blocks with newly cut logs over them

Reverend John and Lee Anna Samuels of Nicodemus, Kansas.
University of Kansas Library

and studied books donated by William Kirtley, a former slave from Kentucky. Mrs. Fletcher taught the children literature, arithmetic, moral values, and hygiene. The school term ranged from three to six months and began in the winter after the harvest. Mrs. Fletcher's school was the first in (the yet-to-be-named) Graham County.

In 1887, Nicodemus had four dry goods stores, three grocery stores, three drugstores, two millinery stores, one land company, one bank, four hotels, two livery stables, two newspapers, two blacksmith shops, two barbers, a shoe shop, two agricultural implement stores, and a two-story schoolhouse costing over $1,000.

But the town was doomed. Development in Nicodemus stopped in late 1888. The town had failed to attract investment capital and the railroad took a different route. With no railroad, people began to move elsewhere. Nicodemus soon became another western ghost town. Residents left for Nebraska and points west seeking new land to homestead.

Men, women, and children of Nicodemus in their wagons.
University of Kansas Library

LULU SADLER CRAIG

Born to former slaves in Missouri in 1868, Lulu Sadler Craig and her family came to Nicodemus, Kansas in 1879. They lived in small dug-out homes, cellars dug deep into the ground, and heated by an iron stove. The stove's smoke pipe sticking out of the earth was the only sign of the dwelling.

During the first winter, Native Americans arrived and offered food they had received from the fort. "Indians didn't give us any trouble," Craig recalled. "Winter was hard to take," she said and without the dug-outs "we would have frozen." Wood was scarce so families had to burn roots and whatever they could find.

No one had a plow so people dug and planted with their hands. Mrs. Craig described how everyone knew one another and pitched in to make Nicodemus a success. Doctors were forty miles away so there were "lots of midwives."

Mrs. Craig, at age fifteen, attended one of Kansas's first schools. She sat in the same classroom as George Washington Carver, who went on to become a famous scientist. She became a teacher and taught in Kansas for forty years. "I did the best I could in those days," she said of the primitive conditions and lack of materials she and her pupils faced.

In 1970, at 102, she celebrated her birthday on her farm surrounded by five generations of Sadlers and Craigs, some 150 relatives and friends in all. Elderly people who lived through lynchings and floggings talked to proud young people with Afros about Malcolm X and the Black Panthers. "Eventually we will come to where we have supposed to have been," said Mrs. Craig.

Pioneer teacher in Kansas and Colorado, Lulu Sadler Craig, on her 102nd birthday. William Loren Katz Collection

CHAPTER 12

TEXAS

Thousands of African-American women lived in Texas as slaves, and after emancipation, most became part of the black poor. Other women arrived as nurses or wives of the Buffalo Soldiers, the black infantrymen, cavalrymen, and Indian scouts for the United States Army.

Some Texas women saw their hopes and dreams fulfilled. In 1888, Laura Owens of Navarro County became the

This beauty parade in Bonham, Texas, around 1910 was a demonstration in black pride. Library of Congress, William Loren Katz Collection

bride of African-American rancher D. W. (80 John) Wallace. The couple built an eight-room ranch home and had four children. Their three girls received college degrees and two of them married professors and taught with them in Texas colleges. A third daughter, educated at Chicago University, became director of Colorado's schools for African Americans. Their son, Carson, also a college graduate, remained on the ranch and looked after the Wallace cattle interests.

LUCY PARSONS

Lucy Gonzales, as much as can be determined, was a mixture of African, Hispanic, and Native American ancestry. Born a slave in 1853 in Texas, she eventually became the country's first significant African-American socialist revolutionary. Her husband, Albert Parsons, was a white man, a former Confederate soldier, and editor of the Waco *Spectator*, an anti–Ku Klux Klan paper. They were an attractive couple and deeply in love.

In 1873, the Parsons no longer felt safe in Texas and left for Chicago. Both soon became embroiled in the drive to form labor unions. They wrote, spoke, and marched for the cause of union labor and social justice. Then, in 1886, Albert Parsons was one of eight union leaders arrested and charged in the Haymarket riot and bombing that left seven police officers dead. Nobody to this day knows who threw the bomb that killed the police officers. While Albert, Lucy, and their two sons were half a mile away having dinner in a tavern, he and the other seven union men were found guilty and sentenced to death. Parsons and three others were executed by the state of Illinois.

Lucy Parsons continued her career as an internationally known radical writer and speaker against injustice based on race, sex, or class. She marched on many picket lines protesting inequality. She died in Chicago in 1943 when a fire swept through her home.

Rhoda [Beaty] was a slave in Jasper County, Texas, who later settled in Travis County. The Institute of Texan Cultures

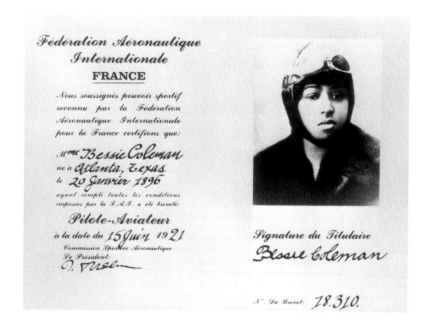

Aviatrix Bessie Coleman, born in Texas, was unable to find a flying instructor in the United States. She gained her French pilot's license in 1921 when she was only 25. The Institute of Texan Cultures

CHAPTER 13

COLORADO'S PIONEERS

A Denver, Colorado, musical family.
Denver Public Library

In 1900, as the African-American population of Colorado grew, urban women of color built a host of societies to fortify them in their daily struggles against bigotry. In Denver they formed the Colored Ladies' Legal Rights Association, the Colored Women's Republican Club, and the Woman's League. In 1901, Augustavia Young, then sixteen, formed the Pond Lily Art and

Children of Colorado miners.
Richardson Collection

Literary Club to challenge the local newspapers' negative images of women of color.

By the early twentieth century, Colorado women had formed clubs for lovers of art, books, and other literary matters. In 1916, four clubs united to establish a day nursery that was still operating in 1992.

These clubs welcomed working and middle-class women. Members generally were married, had children, and most were high school graduates. Many were employed outside their homes as teachers, seamstresses, maids, and musicians. Club meetings were held on weekdays in an effort to encourage attendance by people who as laundresses and domestics worked on Saturdays. In 1904, a Colorado Association of Colored Women's Clubs formed and in four years it represented twelve Denver clubs.

Women also began to march toward political action after 1893, when women's suffrage came to Colorado. In 1906 the Colored Women's Republican Club of Denver, after only five years of effort, proudly announced that a larger percentage of women of color had voted in the recent election than white women. In an age of nationwide segregation, these Denver women had advanced democracy in the West.

At the turn of the century white mobs in southern states lynched three or four men a week. Although African Americans in Colorado were safe from murder, they supported the anti-lynching campaign launched by Tennessee journalist Ida B. Wells in 1892. Then, with the birth of the civil rights organization, the NAACP, in 1909, they contributed money to its anti-lynching efforts as well. Women's clubs also aided orphans, the elderly, and the poor.

By 1910, Colorado's blacks numbered 11,453 (about 1.5 percent of the total population). Most lived in urban centers and almost half were residents of Denver alone.

Women of Boulder's sixty African-American families helped create a vibrant society. "Black women were the backbone of the church, the backbone of the family, they were the backbone of the social life, everything," recalled Dr. Ruth Flowers, born in Boulder in 1902.

World War I was fought "to make the world safe for democracy," but Dr. Flowers pointed out that African Americans in Colorado faced rampant discrimination in

Mrs. Anderson of Leadville, Colorado. William Loren Katz Collection

Some early Colorado pioneers pose for their picture. William Loren Katz Collection

jobs and housing. They were barred from ice-cream parlors, restaurants, movie theaters, even hot-dog stands. The Denver YWCA, so important to the city community, was run on a segregated basis.

Boulder women developed their own alternatives. One was ice-cream socials based on a supply of milk from a Mrs. Harris's Jersey cow. And there were hikes. "We hiked in, I think, every canyon, and every part of the hills," Dr. Flowers recalled. "The mountains were free and we loved them." In 1924 Dr. Flowers, who had worked for many years washing dishes in a restaurant, became the first African-American woman to graduate from the University of Colorado.

RURAL COLORADO

Although the vast majority of African-American women settled in cities, some found happiness in ranch or farm life. Eunice Russell Norris helped take care of the cows, helped build the family log cabin, and kept the household in firewood. When she was sixteen, Marguerite Gomez married a Brighton, Colorado farmer, James Thomas, twice her age and the father of seven children. She learned to herd and break horses and pour medicine down the throats of animals who had become ill. Doris Collins of Rock Spring, despite her mother's strong objections, not only taught herself to ride bareback, but soon surpassed her two brothers in riding horses.

In 1911, seven African-American families, led by Oliver and Minerva Jackson, created an autonomous community in Dearfield, seventy miles east of Denver and thirty miles east of Greely. The Jacksons intended to provide vocational training for African Americans and produce self-sufficient farmers and business people. Minerva Jackson, recalled Irma Ingram, was "the cook, the overseer, everything."

Life was not easy at first, especially for women. Men worked hard in the fields and women labored long in the

Dearfield founder O. T. Jackson holds a young citizen as an unidentified man and woman look on. William Loren Katz Collection

home, with trips to tend the cows and help in the field. "But," recalled resident Sarah Fountain, "they were that kind of women. To make a life, you endure most anything, women do."

Among these early settlers were Hattie Rothwell and her husband, who sold their Denver home and borrowed $500 to homestead in Dearfield. Their son Charles helped Oliver Jackson lay out the town.

Olietta Moore described how her grandmother homesteaded 160 acres in Dearfield, "worked in the fields, raised corn," which they sold in Denver or gave away to friends. Eunice Norris, recalled: "People got along well. It was a peaceful sort of situation: struggling people working hard; they didn't have time for trouble. There was a spirit of helpfulness."

Another woman recalled "moonlight picnics, with lanterns, and big chicken fries. The people were friendly, neighborly."

The Jacksons trumpeted their "valley resort" as having "the best of accommodations," campgrounds for vacationers, and seasonal fishing and hunting. Dearfield had stores, an automobile service, and a gas station. Those ready to take the two-hour car trip could phone and make reservations at its fine restaurant.

Residents were proud of their schools and teachers. They turned out in large numbers to hear and encourage their children's recitations. To finance education, they collected money from neighbors and sometimes from white employers. Sarah Fountain, who arrived in 1918 as a teacher, said,

"I taught them everything in the books and everything I knew." She also organized her students into a church choir and remembered that people there had "a deep respect for teachers."

Dearfield survived even after farm prices collapsed following World War I. But it died during the droughts of the 1930s. One woman recalled, "Most people went out there with high hopes and left with bitter disappointment. It all dried up and blew away."

At a gathering in rural Dearfield, Colorado, well-dressed women and men, including O. T. Jackson on wagon, pose for their photograph. William Loren Katz Collection

CHAPTER 14

NEVADA
WOMEN

In 1859, one of the richest silver veins in the world was discovered on the eastern slopes of the Sierra Nevada mountains. For twenty years this Comstock Lode in Nevada produced millions of dollars and its silver magnet drew adventurous men and women of every color.

During the Civil War, Nevada supported emancipation and after the war it quickly ratified the three Constitutional amendments that ended slavery and granted former slaves equal civil and voting rights.

In 1864, when Nevada's free African-American population began to build a community around their churches and social events, women took a leading role. The birth of Virginia City's First Baptist Church was aided in 1864 by the Ladies Benevolent Association of San Francisco, California, also called the Daughters of Naomi, which presented it with "a magnificent bound pulpit Bible, and one dozen splendid bound hymn books."

First colored baby born in Va. City

The first African-American child born in Virginia City, Nevada. William Loren Katz Collection

Early pioneers in 19th century Reno, Nevada, pose solemnly for their portrait. William Loren Katz Collection

Despite its rapid approval of the three Constitutional amendments after the Civil War, it took years for Nevada to open its schools to all. When it became a state in 1864, the Nevada legislature passed a law denying children of color— "Negroes, Mongolians and Indians"—admission to public schools.

Black residents immediately began to register protests. One of the state's first, wealthiest, and most articulate African-American citizens, Thomas Detter, was an eloquent opposing voice: "We have several colored children here who are growing up in ignorance, all on account of the white man's prejudices. I ask, when will 'man's inhumanity to man' cease?" By 1866, one school welcomed sixteen black children, and another had opened for adults in the evening.

In Carson City, the large African-American population worked diligently to annul the state law. Organized as the Literary and Religious Association of Colored Citizens, its citizens also raised $200 to build their own school and announced, "We value our black babies as well as other folks do theirs."

In 1870, mounting black protests compelled the Elko County School Board to admit children of color. Eventually these children, some of whom had been educated by the African-American community, were admitted to all state public schools.

There were only 396 African-American citizens in the entire state in 1874. Because this small population was widely scattered, social activities were of vital importance to communities. Black women increasingly founded societies to stave off loneliness and isolation and meet their social needs. In 1874 they organized the Dumas Society and Literary Club of Virginia City with twenty-two "ladies and gentlemen." Lecturer Andrew Hall predicted that education would "fit us for positions where caste would be obliterated forever by the brilliancy of our intellectual attainments."

And in that same year in Virginia City prominent residents planned a Grand Calico Ball at the Miners' Union Hall for people from all over western Nevada. For three dollars admission they were served dinner and could dance into the night. In 1877, black women and men formed a literary and social club in Carson City.

Some black women succeeded in business, so much so that in 1874 Mrs. Anna Graham's hairdressing business on C Street in Virginia City, an African-American neighborhood, competed with three other black hairdressing establishments on the same street.

In 1875, Nevada widow Sarah Miner built her husband's express and furniture hauling business into a $6,000 enterprise, lost it in a Virginia city fire, then rebuilt it the next year.

By 1880, most African-American children in Nevada attended school. But then, in the early 1900s, the town of Rawhide prided itself in having driven off people of color and in Fallon whites posted a large sign that read "No Niggers or Japs allowed." In Reno, in 1904, Police Chief Leeper arrested and deported all unemployed African Americans and his policy was endorsed by both daily papers.

Unidentified ladies, Reno, Nevada.
William Loren Katz Collection

CHAPTER 15

SHAPING COMMUNITY IN OKLAHOMA

The Sutton family, Oklahoma homesteaders. Richardson Collection

The Oklahoma Territory had been set aside by the federal government as a permanent home for Native American nations. Thousands of Indians had been marched to Oklahoma on the Trail of Tears. But by 1889, with little cheap land in the west available for white settlement, citizens demanded that Congress open Oklahoma to settlement. Congress agreed, though this drove Native Americans from their land, violating promises and treaties.

At high noon on April 22, 1889, Army guns barked and 100,000 women, men, and children of every color rushed for Oklahoma land. All was dust and excitement, wild horses and overturned carts, breathless and overheated pioneers.

Two million acres of the Oklahoma land taken from Indians was opened to settlement. By nightfall, Oklahoma City had 10,000 citizens in tents and Guthrie had almost 15,000. In both towns, businesses opened the next morning. In a few weeks both had civil governments.

Oklahoma's Cherokee Teachers Institute, held at the Cherokee Female Seminary at Tahlequal around 1890, had students of three different races. William Loren Katz Collection

Congress continued to open more Indian land for eastern settlement—900,000 acres in September 1891; 3,000,000 acres in April 1892. When 6,000,000 acres were opened in September 1893 another 100,000 people lined up.

There were other, smaller rushes and finally, in 1907, a territory once promised to Indians had half a million people and had become the state of Oklahoma. Some 137,000 of its citizens were African Americans. One, Williana Hickman, recalled Oklahoma in 1889: "The family lived in dug-outs. . . .The scenery to me was not at all inviting, and I began to cry."

African Americans had long hoped the Indian Territory might become their refuge from oppression in the southern states. In May 1890, the dynamic, ambitious promoter, Edwin P. McCabe and his family arrived in Oklahoma from Kansas. He had a unique vision for his people. "I expect to have a Negro population of over 100,000 within two years in Oklahoma. . .[and] we will have a Negro state governed by Negroes," the *New York Times* reported him as saying in February 1891. He sent his agents into the South with railroad tickets and brochures promoting homesteads in Oklahoma.

Large African-American groups, sometimes a hundred at a time, with strong family and kinship ties, organized departures for Oklahoma from the Deep South. For women, these unified arrangements provided an invaluable support network on the way and upon arrival.

Since artisans, merchants, professionals, and leaders arrived at the same time, building did not have to wait for various skilled people. Settlement was able to move swiftly. As settlers began to build a new community, family ties and common goals assured there would be cooperation and a minimum of conflict.

An Oklahoma music class prepares for a pageant in the 1890s.
William Loren Katz Collection

White frontier communities were not so lucky. In these settlements, artisans and professionals arrived at different times, sometimes years apart. Individuals with separate agendas often prevented the kind of unified beginning many African-American communities enjoyed.

An early Oklahoma class that served children of three races and both sexes. William Loren Katz Collection

Guthrie, Oklahoma teachers around 1890. University of Oklahoma

LANGSTON CITY

The major black town built after the first Oklahoma Land Rush was Langston City, named after attorney John Mercer Langston, recently elected to Congress from Virginia. By March 1891, its one hundred settlers had twenty frame buildings completed and another dozen started. In the next few months, Edwin McCabe and his agents, who made Langston their headquarters, sold lots to over 150 more families. Langston City consciously sought to attract upwardly mobile, middle-class citizens with community spirit, goods, and some capital. "Come prepared," it advised potential settlers.

Langston City's local paper, the *Herald*, soon boasted a circulation of four thousand readers, larger than any other paper in Oklahoma. It was "one of the neatest printed, ablest edited newspapers in Oklahoma" wrote the white *Yukon Courier*.

By 1892, Langston City had six hundred people from twenty different states. The *Herald* boasted that Langston City was a town of "homes, churches and schools, where you can raise your family in good and respectable society." Three white businessmen and their families were among the residents.

The *Herald* emphasized middle-class values and Victorian chivalry toward women. Men were sternly told to give their church seats to women. The *Herald* asked, "How do you expect other races to respect our ladies when you fail to do so yourselves?" The town founders outlawed prostitution and gambling and serious crimes were unknown within its borders.

Large audiences turned out to hear talks by Bishop Henry M. Turner, who proposed an exodus to Africa, and crusading journalist Ida B. Wells, who demanded an end to lynching. Later, famous white Populist orator Mary E. Lease addressed a huge Langston City meeting.

From the beginning, Langstonians, particularly its women, embraced education with a passion. The nearby Catholic Holy Name College, which also had whites and Indians in its first-grade to high school–grade classes, began to accept African Americans, and in a few years they constituted a majority of the student body.

In 1892, town officials began a tax-supported public school with classes up to the eighth grade. As students graduated, a new high school was begun, its governing board announcing acceptance of students "regardless of race, color or number." In 1892, some of Langston City's founders and their wives decided to make their town the educational center of black Oklahoma.

The educational efforts of the town's early women and men led to spectacular victories. By 1900, Langston City boasted a literacy rate among the highest of any frontier community in the United States: 72 percent of its citizens could read and 70 percent could write. For Langston City's pioneer women between the ages of fifteen and forty-five, the figures were even higher—96 percent could read and 95 percent could write.

BOLEY

Boley was founded in September 1904 on eighty acres owned by Abigail Barnett, a young African-American woman with Choctaw ancestors. It soon became the largest predominantly African-American town in the West. By March 1905, it had a newspaper, the *Boley Progress*, to sing its

A young woman stands in front of the Le Grand residence in Boley, Oklahoma. Oklahoma Historical Society

praises and to offer the upbeat motto, "All Men Up—Not Some Men Down."

The *Progress* appeared just in time to welcome trainloads of settlers who arrived in the next two years. In April 1905, Boley had 400 settlers, by November the figure reached 750, and four months later it was up to 800.

Streets were dusty and living conditions were primitive. But within a few months Boley had a general store, a hardware store, a drugstore, a hotel, a sawmill, and a cotton gin. Then citizens built a community structure, 24 feet by 40 feet, to serve as a school and a church. On weekdays two teachers instructed 150 children. On Sundays, Methodists held services in the morning and Baptists in the afternoon. The town boasted a Women's Club, Union Literary Society, and Odd Fellows Hall.

Boley's religions soon outgrew a single community building. With its women taking the lead, the town soon had four congregations. By 1906, Baptists had built their own church. In a short while four different houses of worship had been built.

Social activities such as parties, balls, dinners, and wedding receptions—organized by women—flowed from church associations. The *Progress* advised women to stress community uplift, discipline children, and "manage your husbands and see the results."

Education was Boley's pride and the results were gratifying. Half of its high school students went on to college. School attendance for black girls exceeded that of boys.

Rigid lines did not separate men from women. Boley women spoke at public meetings and helped set and meet community goals. When James Thompson formed the Patriarchs of America, he invited both sexes to join, and women participated in meetings, read papers, and led discussion groups.

However, women felt the need for separate societies. Thompson's wife, Neva Thompson, created the Sisters of Ethiopia, the Alpha Club, and a Thompson Literary Society. The "United Brotherhood of Friends and Sisters Mysterious 10" built a home for the elderly and orphans and another club collected money for a local woman who was destitute.

The women of Oklahoma struck an independent note and achieved a level of equality that had to be the envy of their sisters elsewhere.

A Fort Gibson, Oklahoma store run by women and men in the 1890s. William Loren Katz Collection

CHAPTER 16

SUCCEEDING IN SEATTLE

In 1898, Mrs. May B. Mason, a widow, rushed to the Yukon alone and returned to Seattle with $5,000 in gold dust and a land claim. Esther Mumford Collection

Susan Revels met Horace Cayton, ten years older than her, when they were students at Alcorn College, Mississippi, where her father Hiram Revels was the president. After Cayton left for a journalism job in Utah, she corresponded with him and sent along her own writing efforts, short stories, and news articles.

In 1896, the two were reunited and married in Seattle, where she became the twenty-fifth African-American woman in a town of forty-two-thousand people. By then some African Americans had lived on the Pacific coast for generations.

Horace Cayton owned a newspaper, the *Republican*. It did so well the newlyweds soon moved to a comfortable home on Capitol Hill, an affluent neighborhood, and began a family. With few people of color nearby, whites in Seattle, Portland, Oregon, and other cities of the Pacific Northwest did not insist on segregated neighborhoods.

Susan Cayton contributed articles to the *Republican*, and soon became its assistant editor. In 1900, the white Seattle *Post-Intelligencer* began to publish her articles as well. The Caytons became the most prominent African-American family in Seattle. Her son, Horace, Jr., later a noted writer, remembered neighbors being "pleasant and respectful."

Horace, Jr. recalled his mother as well bred, graceful, "tall, and of a stately bearing." She had the "warm earthiness of my Methodist grandfather and the tight primness of my Quaker grandmother." Mrs. Cayton became a leading member of black Seattle's upper class. She started the Dorcas Charity Club for African-American women and made sure her children took music lessons, visited the opera, and saw Shakespearean plays. The Caytons had a young Japanese servant named Nish. Susan Cayton taught him English in exchange for lessons in Japanese.

Black women in Seattle did not appear in the census data until 1879. That year the city listed nine African-American women. Mary Stevens, who had been born in Africa, lived with her family on a farm in the Cedar Mountain area of King County. Most of the other twenty-four women in the 1891 census were nurses or housekeepers. Annie Jackson was a music teacher. One woman remembered her sad arrival: "There were few of our own people living in Seattle when we came in 1889 and at times I got very lonely." Solitude and isolation were constant problems for all women, but more so for women of color.

Miss Sara Elizabeth Massender arrived in Seattle, Washington, in 1899 from British Columbia. Esther Mumford Collection

Children of color were reminded by their mothers to be "a credit to the race." Correct speech was watched over in the home by the more educated parents, often the wife who, as historian Esther Mumford wrote, had been educated in freedmen's schools set up in the South after the Civil War.

In 1886, Mrs. Theresa Brown Dixon, who had attended nursing school, became a Seattle nurse and midwife. Her two daughters also became professional nurses and worked in the area for more than thirty years.

A few women of color were hired in Seattle offices. In 1899, Clara Threet enrolled in Leo's Business College, graduated, and was hired part-time by a white attorney. By 1901, she was working full-time as a stenographer. Her sister followed in her footsteps, but many other young black women

Mrs. Sarah Grose (left), who arrived in Seattle in 1860, may have been the first African-American woman resident of the town. Esther Mumford Collection

who had professional training were rejected by both large companies and small offices. Some women and men worked in the hop fields east and west of the Cascade Mountains in the fall, alongside Indian, Chinese, Japanese, and white laborers.

In 1889, the Ladies Colored Social Circle formed. They held weekly meetings in wealthy homes and planned literary, musical, and entertainment events for their community. In the 1890s, women of color joined the National Afro-American Council to promote the political interests of their people. Elizabeth Oxindine recalled that era in the town: "There was something going on all the time. Balls, barbecues, picnics, excursions. There was always some place to go."

A leading center of middle-class social activity was the African Methodist Episcopal (AME) Church. The other was the home of early settlers William and Sarah Grose, who turned Sunday into feast day, serving chicken, duck, and pork, vegetables, cakes, pies, berries, and other fruit. By 1901, Seattle's African-American community had also founded a Music Club and an Evergreen Literary Society.

The annual celebration of Emancipation Day, the day President Lincoln signed the Emancipation Proclamation to free slaves in the South, drew people together from every economic class. Many African Americans attended cake-walks, baseball contests, and evening Shakespeare performances.

African-American children in Seattle attended desegregated schools, but some had to contend with bigoted teachers. In 1900 in Seattle's Pacific School, Theresa Flowers felt "great prejudice. They'd call you names." In the Warren Avenue school that Mattie Harris and her brother attended, white pupils accepted her brother but she felt "I had no chance."

Elsewhere in the Pacific Northwest, small communities sprouted around African-American churches. In Portland, Oregon, a black congregation in 1862 formed a "People's Church" and in 1883 the town had a black Methodist Episcopal Church. By the turn of the century 775 African-American women and men, 65 percent of the state's people of color, called Portland home. With growing numbers and determined agitation, by 1880 they had defeated the school segregation imposed in 1867. Black children were taught by white teachers and in classes surrounded by white faces.

CHAPTER 17

ALMOST ALONE

Mr. Howard Kerr, who served in U. S. 10th Cavalry,
was photographed with his wife. Richardson Collection.

African Americans who traveled to sparsely settled Rocky Mountain states found few other people of color. In 1900, Montana had 1,523, including 611 women, North Dakota had 286 with 113 women, South Dakota had 465 men with 193 women, and Wyoming had 940 with 309 women.

In these remote locations, black women often felt like a dark island surrounded by a white sea. To stem a feeling of loneliness and combat a sense of isolation, some created unique responses.

African Americans arrived in Helena, Montana before it was organized as a U.S. territory and when it was still called Last Chance Gulch. A black was among the three

In 1924 delegates to the Montana Federation of Colored Women's Clubs assembled in Bozeman. Montana Historical Society

who discovered gold near Helena in 1862. In 1867, enough black people had arrived to constitute a church congregation and in 1888 they formed the St. James Church. The next year, as Montana became a state, the African Methodist Episcopal church congregation had a building.

In 1872, the territorial legislature, over the vigorous protests of people of color, passed a segregated school law. For the next ten years, aided by some whites, black citizens battled the laws and in 1882 finally ended segregated schools.

The African-American population slowly rose after the Civil War, but always remained a tiny minority. In 1870, Helena's black population was 71, or 2.3 percent of the total; by 1910 it reached its high of 420 or 3.4 percent of the 12,515 people in Helena.

Black women pursued their own interests and often took an independent stance. They formed such clubs as the Busy Bees and Willen Workers to raise funds for churches or help the unfortunate. From 1906 to 1911, the black community's

Unidentified women pioneers from Blair Colony, South Dakota (above) and
Wyoming (below). South Dakota Archives and Wyoming State Museum

Unidentified early Wyoming pioneer. Wyoming State Museum

newspaper, the *Montana Plaindealer*, bravely advocated equal rights. In 1880, an "Afro-American Building Association" in Helena promoted real estate and business among people of color. Of its eight managers, three were women: Mary Mathews, Mattie Simmons, and Lenora Johnson, two of whom owned their own concerns.

In 1911, the *Plaindealer* featured an article by citizen Annie Walton that denounced prejudice in Montana. She insisted that northern bigotry generally is "as intense as that in the south" and more hypocritical. She urged black people to unite, practice self-help, and to seek economic independence.

Melissa Boulware, born to a Choctaw father and an African-American mother in 1866, had a fourth-grade education and read and wrote with difficulty. In Missouri she had met Silas Smith, a white man who had been a scout for the army during the Indian wars and had resigned after 1876. They married and joined a wagon train to Cheyenne, Wyoming.

Smith filed a claim on 160 acres in Wyoming twenty-five years before it became a state. In 1893, the family, which included nine children, moved to a 1700-acre ranch in Chugwater near Cheyenne. The family also owned another ranch east of Casper. By 1906, Melissa Smith and her older daughters were cooking on working days for at least sixteen laborers at the ranch.

Mrs. Smith saw that her children attended the African Methodist Church in Cheyenne. She dressed the girls for services in starched shirtwaists with lace-trimmed jackets and dark-pleated skirts and the boys in Buster Brown suits. When her son Nolle graduated from high school but did not want to run the Chugwater ranch as his father wanted, his mother conspired with him so he could attend college.

Melissa Smith was ninety-nine when she died in Hawaii in 1965, where she lived with her son Nolle. She had watched Nolle marry a Hawaiian woman and win election to the territorial legislature in a district that had less than a dozen black people.

Wyoming had less than one thousand African Americans when it became a state in 1890. Girls and boys of all races took part in school, sleigh rides, and parties. Mixed groups attended the city's opera house to enjoy plays and Buffalo Bill's Wild West Show. However, in Cheyenne, Sudie Rhone found that women of color did not feel welcome in clubs formed by white women. In 1904, African-American women began their own Searchlight Club.

Elsewhere in frontier communities, many a young person had to adjust to being the only black student in a class or school. Future writer Era Bell Thompson grew up in North Dakota. She was one of only 236 black women in the state. She recalled neighbors who befriended her parents and a Norwegian family who brought them supplies at critical times. "I was very lucky to have grown up in North Dakota," she said, "where families were busy fighting climate and soil for a livelihood and there was little awareness of race."

Thompson became a track star at North Dakota State University and later pursued a career as a journalist. As "Dakota Dick," she wrote a column on "the wild and wooly west" for the *Chicago Defender*. An early editor of *Ebony*, she did much to make it the most successful African-American magazine in history. She went on to write three books. Her biography, *American Daughter* (1945), described her teenage life on the frontier.

Other women were able to make their mark on the frontier by sheer will, even when they felt most alone. In 1908, Mrs. Daisy O'Brien Rudisell gave birth to her son William, the first African-American child born in Alaska's Yukon. If she felt isolated at that moment, it was understandable. There were only a handful of African Americans in the Alaska Territory at the time. And she was the only person in the tent hospital who was not white. William entered the world as winds howled and the temperature plunged to fifty-two degrees below zero outside.

Some African-American women went west to take jobs as cooks or maids for wives of U.S. Army officers. At remote Army posts with few other African Americans around, they found life could be lonely and often disappointing. One black cook, Eliza, bemoaned her fate: "I hain't got nobody and there ain't no picnics nor church sociables nor no buryings out here."

Although African-American officers in the U.S. military were few—in 1892 only three chaplains and two second lieutenants—some of their wives bravely accompanied them to distant posts.

In 1896, Infantry Chaplain Theophilus Steward married Dr. Susan McKinney, a widow and a woman of varied and unique talents. McKinney was the first African-American woman physician in New York State and only the third in the United States. A bold defender of black womanhood, she strongly advocated women joining the medical profession. When she accompanied her husband to Fort Missoula, Montana, she earned a state license to practice medicine there.

Dr. Steward also accompanied her husband to Texas and Fort Niobrara, Nebraska. "Dr. Susan" was more than welcome wherever she went. Besides her healing abilities, she had a fine knowledge of music. Nebraska townspeople, her husband reported, "were friendly and we often shared the Christian hospitality of the good Methodist families." She "was very useful among the ladies of the Women's Christian Temperance Union, her skill in music and knowledge of medicine making her of important service to them." In 1905, she organized ten enlisted men into a Christmas Eve choir that gave "an excellent program." Two years later she traveled to Haiti to deliver her first grandson, Louis Holly.

After his retirement from the Army, the Stewards twice visited Europe, once for pleasure in 1909, and again in 1911 so Dr. Susan M. Steward could present a paper on African-American women at the Universal Races Conference in London. When she died in 1919, in Brooklyn, New York, her funeral oration was delivered by one of her strongest admirers, Dr. W. E. B. Du Bois, the greatest African-American scholar of the century.

SOUTH DAKOTA LEGENDS

Although in 1862 the Dakota territorial legislature had narrowly voted down a bill "to prevent persons of color [from] residing in Dakota," by 1868 black males had been granted the right to vote there. In 1870, the territory's population of thirteen thousand included only ninety-four black people. Most had settled east of the Missouri river in Yankton, Buffalo, and Bon Homme counties.

In 1874, Lieutenant George Custer's expedition into the Dakotas included a black cook, Sarah Campbell. The discovery of gold drew others and by 1880, four hundred people

Susan McKinney Stewart, the first woman physician in New York City, accompanied her husband to Fort Missoula, Montana, and Fort Niobrara, Nebraska. Schomburg Center for Research in Black Culture

of color lived in Dakota. In 1875, when black miners struck it rich in Lawrence County, their land was called "Nigger Hill." Another nearby strike by black miners brought out $1,700 in gold in one day and was soon called "Nigger Gulch."

Rising racial antagonism forced African Americans to settle in isolated areas near Onida and Yankton. Former slave settlers of Yankton built one of the oldest churches in the state in 1885 (founded in 1883), the African Methodist Episcopal Church (506 Cedar Street) and used it for more than a hundred years. Today it is the home of the Black History Museum. In 1890 Yankton had sixty-two residents of color.

Mrs. Cornelia Garrett came to Huron, Dakota, in 1880 as a cook on the railroad, settled down, and lived to be 111 years old. Others—several hundred in Onida, Sully County—farmed, raised livestock, fished, and hunted game and, recalled one, "survived the first winter or two in their sod homes or dugouts just like the other settlers did."

The Chapman family who arrived in Yankton in the 1880s included young Kate born in 1870. At age nineteen she was called "one of the literary lights of the race." Frail and plagued by childhood diseases, she was taught by her mother, a former schoolteacher, and did not attend school until she was twelve. At thirteen she wrote her first poem, "A Dying Child's Fantasy." Her poem, "Memory," appeared in the *Christian Recorder* and attracted favorable attention.

In 1889, one of Chapman's poems appeared on the front page of the *Indianapolis Freeman*, a popular black weekly. It praised the patience, courage, and perseverance of black people in the face of bigotry and hate and urged them to "stand firmly as a race" and drive injustice from the land. It ended: "the darkest night gives way to the brightest day." "My work as a writer has barely begun," she rejoiced.

In 1890, Chapman contributed to *Our Women and Children*, a magazine edited by black scholar William J. Simmons. She said her ambition was to become "to the girls of our race what Mrs. Alcott . . . and hosts of other women have been to theirs." Though her illness often interrupted her efforts, she continued to write both prose and poetry.

Black settlers such as Ted Blakey's family, who operated a successful truck garden business, promoted Yankton to people of color back east. He said: "My people used to tell others: 'Come to South Dakota and you will experience freedom like you never had before.'"

CHAPTER 18

MARY FIELDS OF CASCADE, MONTANA

Mary Fields, known as Stagecoach Mary or Black Mary, was one of the toughest characters to stride the northern Rockies near Cascade, Montana. She was six foot, two hundred pounds, and carried a .38 Smith and Wesson strapped under her apron. She was reputed to be a crack shot who did not miss a target within fifty paces.

Gary Cooper, the actor, knew her as a young boy and idolized her. "I remember seeing her in Cascade when I was just a little shaver of nine or so. She smoked cigars until the day she died in 1914. She must have been about eighty-one." Western artist Charles Russell made a sketch of her and as late as 1959 the Russell portrait hung in a Cascade bank.

Mary Fields was born a slave in Tennessee during the presidency of Andrew Jackson. In Toledo, Ohio, after the Civil War, she met Mother Amadeus of the Ursuline Convent and became her personal servant. In 1881 Mother Amadeus left for St. Peter's Mission in Montana to open a school for Blackfeet Indian girls and women.

Fields did not accompany her, but in 1884, when Mother Amadeus fell ill with pneumonia, Fields left for Cascade to nurse her back to health in her log cabin. When Fields decided to stay on, she was given the job of delivering freight for the mission. One night when a pack of wolves frightened her horses and her load overturned, she guarded it through the night. On another night, a blizzard kept her from following the road and she had to walk back and forth to keep from freezing.

Mary Fields feared no one and occasionally let her temper erupt. During her ten years at the Mission, the bishop heard one complaint after another about her. The final straw came when she and a cowpuncher had a shootout. No one was hurt, but the bishop directed Mother Amadeus to fire her.

With Mother Amadeus's help, she set up a restaurant in Cascade but she twice went broke. Next the holy mother helped Fields land the mail route between the mission and Cascade. "Each day, never missing a one," Cooper reported, "she made her triumphant entry into the mission seated on top of the mail coach dressed in a man's hat and coat and smoking a huge cigar." She became only the second American woman to drive a U.S. mail route.

For the next eight years, "Stagecoach" Mary carried the mail. In her only mishap, she was thrown from the mail coach and had to be nursed by the sisters at the mission.

In 1903, Fields lived in Cascade, took in washing, and ran a laundry. One day when she was about seventy and was having a drink in the saloon, a male customer who had refused to pay a $2 laundry bill walked by. She trotted after him, tapped him on the shoulder, and when he turned around she knocked him out with a single punch. Back at the saloon she announced, "His laundry bill is paid."

In these early years of the 1900s, Fields was adored by Cascade's young and old, and children gathered to celebrate her birthday. When the owner of the local hotel leased it to another, it was with the understanding that Mary Fields would still receive her meals free. In 1912, when her laundry was destroyed by fire, townspeople donated lumber and their labor to build her a new one.

Decades later, Gary Cooper characterized his idol: "Mary was one of the melting pot of pioneers, black, white and yellow who came from Tennessee and places beyond the seas to help conquer and tame the old Wild West. When she died the town mourned her passing and they buried her at the foot of the mountains, by the winding road that leads to the old mission."

Stagecoach Mary Fields in typical garb. William Loren Katz Collection

THEY MADE
A DIFFERENCE

To find their American dream on the frontier, African-American women trudged all the wilderness trails. Some slaves fled westward on foot and others sued their masters in court. Many bumped along in Conestoga wagons, prairie schooners that forded rivers, climbed mountains, and often broke down. Some reached the Ohio Valley, and others rolled into the sod house frontier of Kansas and Nebraska. Some arrived later in the southwest, the mountain states, and the Pacific far west by iron horse or stagecoach. Life for these women was never easy and sometimes it was downright dangerous.

Tens of thousands of African-American women grew up as members of proud Indian nations ready to fight for land

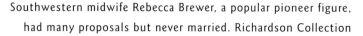
Southwestern midwife Rebecca Brewer, a popular pioneer figure, had many proposals but never married. Richardson Collection

they knew was theirs. Thousands of others held their skirts above their ankles as they, their husbands, and brothers, raced unceremoniously for homesteads in Oklahoma. Still others were part of the gold fever that struck California, Alaska, and Colorado.

Some women of color traveled with their families or sometimes alone looking for a good job, a loving husband, some land they could call their own—the new life the West promised Americans. They ran more than households and families. They also ran laundries, hotels, farms, and carting

Mariana Billingsly and her pioneer family in the southwest.
Richardson Collection

Mary Woods Wilson, early southwestern settler.
Richardson Collection

Homesteaders near Brownlee,
Cherry County, Nebraska.
William Loren Katz Collection

firms. Others taught school, scrubbed floors, wrote for newspapers, or herded cattle and horses. Their frontier grit helped transform dismal, sparsely settled territories into thriving, populous states.

Then these pioneers stayed on to become poets and cooks, journalists and civil rights agitators, schoolteachers and cowgirls, nurses and homesteaders. They worked alongside their men in western fields, stores, and offices. Even when they were loaded down with all the household chores and family responsibilities, few ever thought of themselves as just mothers or housewives. To fend off loneliness in the wilderness, they mastered the art of self-help associations.

African-American women found the time after a hard day's work to devote their energies to spiritual and economic uplift for their people. They built schools and churches, created cultural institutions, and organized community activities. Day into night they poured themselves into the hearty fellowship and trying labor that kept communities afloat. Their social and cultural activities kept the blood of family and community life pumping.

Above all, these pioneer Americans, even if it meant building churches and schools stone by stone, saw that their children were educated. If not their time, then at least their children's time had come, they insisted. These women demanded that their daughters and sons improve their minds at home, pay attention to their lessons in class, and prepare themselves for the new opportunities offered by the farthest ranges of the land of the free.

Their boundless spirit and strength, and uncommon courage, did more than create charitable, literary, and religious societies. Along the way, the African-American women of the West challenged American bigotry and provided white citizens with vital and sometimes painful lessons in the value of democracy, justice, and liberty for all. Their herculean efforts sometimes broke down ancient walls and opened doors for their children.

Their monuments can still be found in old churches, libraries, museums, and homes. These monuments pay silent tribute to the trials, tenacity, and bravery of a people who, a long way from home, struggled for their dream in the old West.

An attractive Western settler identified only as "Chloe." William Loren Katz Collection

Early Nebraska pioneer. Nebraska State Historical Society

ANNOTATED BIBLIOGRAPHY

Asbaugh, Carolyn. *Lucy Parsons, American Revolutionary.* Chicago: Kerr Company, 1976, is the story of the Texas-born life-long radical.

Bruyn, Kathleen. *"Aunt" Clara Brown.* Boulder, Colorado: Pruett Publishing Company, 1970, is the story of the generous Colorado pioneer.

DeGraff, Larence B. "Race, Sex and Regions: Black Women in the American West." *Pacific Historical Review* (May 1980), 285-313, is a pioneering study of the subject.

Hamilton, Kenneth M. *Black Towns and Profit.* Chicago: University of Illinois Press, 1991, includes material on women in Kansas and Oklahoma.

Hine, Darlene Clark, ed. *Black Women in America: An Historical Encyclopedia.* Brooklyn, New York: Carlson Publishing Inc., 1933. This big, two-volume work includes biographies of some western African-American women and special articles on the "Northwest Territory," "Western Territories," "Kansas Federation of Colored Women's Clubs," "Oakland, California Black Women's Clubs," and the "Denver, Colorado Club Movement."

Katz, William Loren. *The Black West.* New York: Simon & Schuster (forthcoming, 1996), includes short biographies of certain figures and devotes a full chapter to each subject.

———. "Pioneer Sisters," *Essence* (February 1994) is an effort to synopsize and describe this frontier experience with old photographs.

Mumford, Esther Hale. *Seattle's Black Victorians, 1852-1901.* Seattle: Anase Press, 1980, is a fine study of one city with the emphasis on its women.

Painter, Nell Irvin. *Exodusters.* New York: Norton, 1976, is the best full-scale study of the Exodus of 1879 and its women participants.

INDEX